I0814532

21ST Century Skills INNOVATION LIBRARY | Design a Better World

A Better Alarm System

Peter Pasque

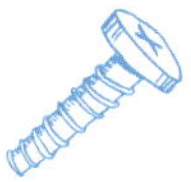

Published in the United States of America by Cherry Lake Publishing
Ann Arbor, Michigan
www.cherrylakepublishing.com

Content Adviser: Kristin Fontichiaro, University of Michigan School of Information, Ann Arbor, MI
Reading Adviser: Marla Conn MS, Ed., Literacy specialist, Read-Ability, Inc.

Photo Credits: © Dmitry Veryovkin/Shutterstock.com, cover, 1; © ruslanPhoto/Shutterstock.com, 5; © Volodymyr Maksymchuk/Shutterstock.com, 6; © Trong Nguyen/Shutterstock.com, 7; © Ani Estel/Shutterstock.com, 8; © Monkey Business Images/Shutterstock.com, 11; © Nyyencha/Shutterstock.com, 12; © SergeyKlopotov/Shutterstock.com, 13; © leungchopan/Shutterstock.com, 15; © Dmytro Zinkevych/Shutterstock.com, 21; © loraks/Shutterstock.com, 23; © Alex_Traksel/Shutterstock.com, 25

Graphic Element Credits: © Ohn Mar/Shutterstock.com, back cover, multiple interior pages; © Dmitrieva Katerina/Shutterstock.com, back cover, multiple interior pages; © advent/Shutterstock.com, back cover, front cover, multiple interior pages; © Visual Generation/Shutterstock.com, multiple interior pages; © anfisa focusova/Shutterstock.com, front cover, multiple interior pages; © Babich Alexander/Shutterstock.com, back cover, front cover, multiple interior pages

Library of Congress Cataloging-in-Publication Data

Names: Pasque, Peter, author.
Title: A better alarm system / by Peter Pasque.
Description: Ann Arbor : Cherry Lake Publishing, [2019] | Series: Design a better world | Includes bibliographical references and index. | Audience: Grade 4 to 6.
Identifiers: LCCN 2018037691| ISBN 9781534143241 (hardcover) | ISBN 9781534141001 (pdf) | ISBN 9781534139800 (pbk.) | ISBN 9781534142206 (hosted ebook)
Subjects: LCSH: Electric alarms–Juvenile literature.
Classification: LCC TK7241 .P37 2019 | DDC 621.389/28–dc23
LC record available at https://lccn.loc.gov/2018037691

Printed in the United States of America
Corporate Graphics

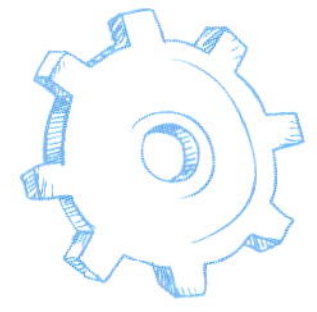

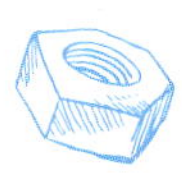

Table of Contents

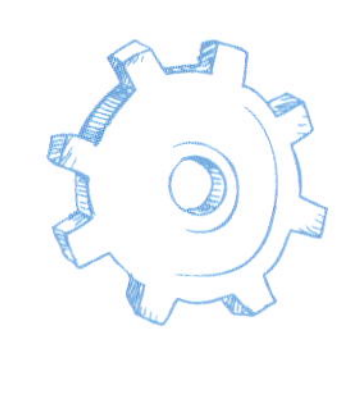

CHAPTER ONE

Design Thinking and Identifying a Problem

Have you ever had an idea so great it could solve a problem for you or someone else? Maybe your idea could make someone's life easier or better! **Makers** have these ideas all the time—they even design and build some of them. Being a maker is cool and can lead you into the world of professional **designers** called engineers. And if you get good at electronics, you may want to explore the field of **electrical engineering**.

Are you the type of person who wonders how **electricity** makes fan blades move? Or how the batteries in a flashlight make the light come on? You can use electric components to solve a problem in your own life. One of the cool things about electronic experiments is that solutions can be simple or complex—the difficulty will depend on your design and your experience level with electronics. If you are new to electronics, you may start by solving problems with a simple circuit and a switch. Once you have a lot of experience with electronics, you might build a sensor that transmits a signal over the internet.

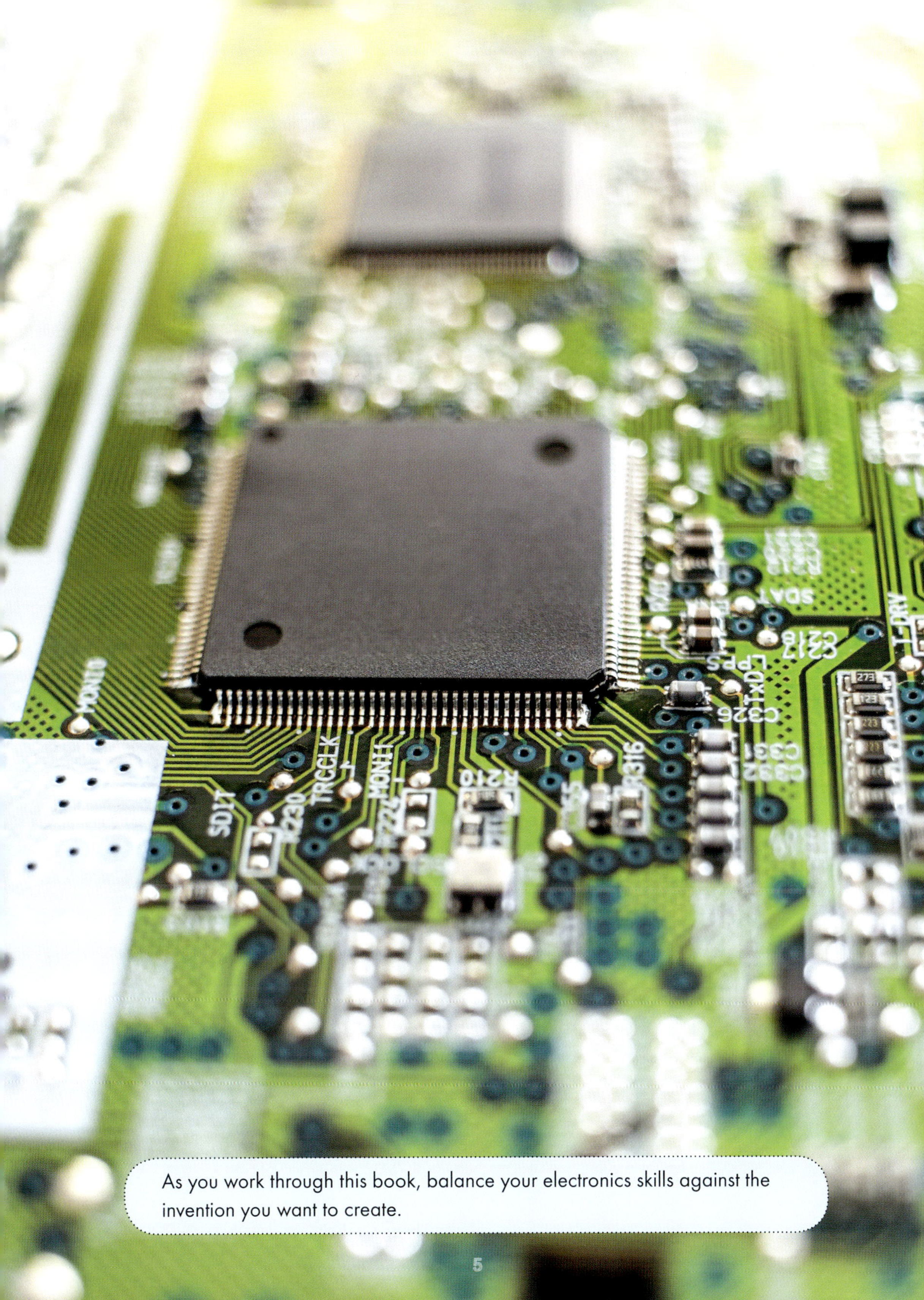

As you work through this book, balance your electronics skills against the invention you want to create.

The design problem we will use in this book is: How do I keep my snooping sibling out of my stuff?

Do you wish you had a way to keep something private? You know, *your* stuff—the things that you consider treasures—private? Maybe you have a diary, drawings, or a special toy that you'd like to keep private. You could complain to your parents that someone has been snooping in your stuff again. Or you could take matters into your own hands and invent a solution! Engineers call this a **design problem**.

Everyone's special stuff is different and will require different techniques to secure. Makers, engineers, and problem solvers often use a specific way of organizing thoughts around solving a design problem. In the world of designers and inventors, this system is called **design thinking**. A very innovative company called IDEO first created design thinking as a method of solving problems. Now, people all over the world use design thinking to improve inventions, activities, and even schools! An important

Design thinking can help find ways to improve the things you use every day. How might you improve a bicycle?

A diary or journal is private—you want to keep it safe!

idea used in design thinking is that the people with the problem are the most important ones to consult when trying to solve that problem.

Let's explore design thinking to solve the problem of keeping your special stuff secure. See if you can create a snooping sibling alarm.

Try This

Find something you'd like to keep private. Maybe it's a diary, sketchpad, or little box of treasures. Think about how often you use it. Is this something you need easy access to? How big is your treasure? Is it fragile?

Next, think about how you want to secure it. Do you want to use a loud alarm to scare the snooping person away? Or do you want use a silent alarm, so only you can tell if someone has snooped? Do you want to lock it up so snooping is difficult or develop some other method? List all the possible issues surrounding the design problem that you can think of. You will use this list in your journey to design your very own snooping sibling alarm!

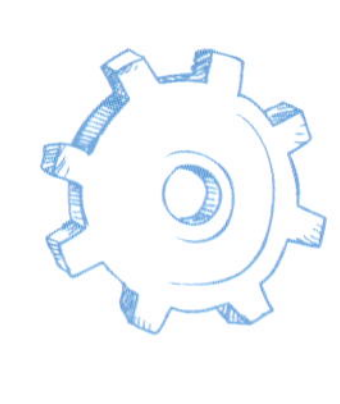

Research, Observe, and Interview

Your list of issues is the first step in finding a solution to your design thinking process. Now let's start collecting data.

Research

Doing research to learn about electronic circuits and discovering solutions that others have come up with can help you make a better design. Search the internet for "kid designed burglar alarm," "simple circuits for kids," and "electricity experiments for kids." Try using different search terms so you get a wide variety of ideas.

An important part of the design thinking process is to ask experts. They can be people who have the same problem you are trying to solve. Experts should also include librarians and people at your local **makerspace**.

When gathering research from experts, you may want to ask questions such as:

- Can you help me learn how to design a burglar alarm using electronics?

A makerspace is a great place to meet people who are experts on electronics.

Experimenting with circuits can help you become an expert yourself!

- Are there electronics kits I can use to learn more about simple circuits and how electronic components work? Some of these kits might include Snap Circuits, Squishy Circuits, littleBits, or even **microcontrollers** such as an Arduino (shown in photo above).

Ask a lot of questions and experiment as often as you can. The more comfortable you become with how and why electricity flows through a circuit, the more options you will have when solving design problems.

Observe

The power of observation is a key tool in the designer's toolbox. Observe your treasure and look for logical ways to secure it that won't damage or destroy the thing you love. Also, observe the functions of different electronic components and how they work together. Look at your

Observing the way electronic toys work is an important step in creating your own invention.

toys that use simple electronics. See where the **input** sensors are, where the **output** features are, and if there is a feedback loop that changes how the toy behaves in different conditions. If there is a feedback loop, the toy likely has a microcontroller in it.

Some libraries and makerspaces offer sessions where you get to take apart a toy. These sessions will teach you how professional engineers use circuits in toys. If you do get to attend one, be sure to bring your **designer's notebook** to take notes and draw pictures of your observations. You can also take photos with a tablet or smartphone.

Interview

Interview people you know and ask how they secure their treasures. Take notes on important facts, make sketches of ideas, and record the details of your observations. You can ask to see some of their solutions, but don't be disappointed if they decline to show you their secrets. Even so, you can still learn a lot from them by asking careful questions. You could even ask security guards, locksmiths, or security experts about how to keep things safe! Here are some ideas for questions:

- What types of treasures do you need to secure?
- Do you have different ways of securing different types of treasures?
- Have you ever caught anyone snooping in your stuff?
- Have you ever lost something you cared about because you hid it and forgot where you put it?
- What is your favorite way to secure treasures?
- Do you have a burglar alarm? If so, how does it work?

This interviewer is using two great techniques: making notes by hand instead of looking down at a computer, and making eye contact with the interviewee.

Notes

Engineers, designers, and makers take notes in a designer's notebook. These notes should include ideas and research you gather from reading about similar problems and from interviews. It should also include sketches you make during interviews and while reading, as well as descriptions and drawings of the electronic experiments you conduct. Gathering information from people with the same problem you are trying to solve is an important part of design thinking.

Find or make your own designer's notebook for this project. Pro tip: Try and keep your notes spread out on the page and easy to read. Use lots of pictures and don't cram too much information on one piece of paper. You can always get more paper!

Online, look up "**schematic** diagrams for kids" and begin to familiarize yourself with common symbols. Draw and label some of the schematic symbols and diagrams in your notebook.

Try This

1. **Research:** Do a Google search for "kid designed burglar alarm," "simple circuits for kids," and "electricity experiments for kids." Begin building your knowledge base from the search results. Stick to resources for kids until you gain more experience. Next, go to your library or makerspace and experiment with electronic circuits. If you already have experience with circuits, you may want to use search terms like "Arduino" or "microcontrollers."
2. **Observe:** Look at how existing burglar alarms work and how toys use simple circuits in their design. An alarm you may be familiar with is the one in the board game Operation. The alarm buzzes if you touch the tweezers to the patient. See if you can figure out how that alarm works. Searching for "kid burglar alarms" on YouTube is another great place to get new ideas.
3. **Interview:** Conduct at least two interviews with parents, teachers, or relatives, and ask them about strategies they've used to prevent snoopers from peeping at their stuff. Ask if anyone has used an electronic alarm or device to solve this problem and use the suggested questions presented earlier in the chapter.

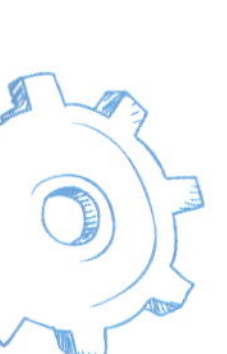

CHAPTER THREE

Synthesize and Focus

Now that you have gathered some research through books, computers, observations, interviews, and experiments, it is time to **synthesize** and **focus** this new knowledge into potential solutions. Read through the notes in your designer's notebook and see if they lead you to the need for more research. When you are satisfied with your notes, identify some of the most useful thoughts and look for **patterns**. You may want to highlight key ideas, make additional notes in the margins, and even take notes on your notes! Synthesizing and focusing your notes includes organizing them by topic.

The patterns you notice can help you focus on the problem you want to solve. Pick the one that you think is the most important or exciting to you. For now, don't worry about solving the problem. You just need to decide what problem you want to solve so you are ready for the next step!

Try This

Put the best ideas on index cards so you can organize them on the table or on a corkboard. Ask yourself these questions (and more):

- What are some of the best solutions the people you interviewed had for securing their stuff and preventing snoopers?
- What would stop *you* from snooping in someone else's stuff?
- What have you learned about simple circuits?
- What are the best low-tech alarm triggers you've uncovered in your research?
- Is there a kit or resource from your library or makerspace that you'd like to use for your project? It is likely your project will be made from things you have around the house or at school.
- Should you design a container for your stuff that includes an alarm or something that alerts you when an intruder has been snooping?

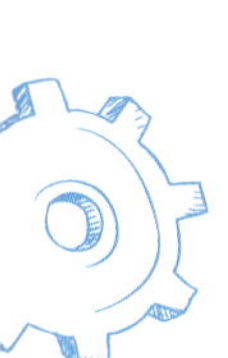

CHAPTER FOUR

Brainstorm

Brainstorming is a process where you and your friends or classmates try to come up with lots of free-flowing ideas for solving a problem. In this example, our design problem is "How do I keep my snooping sibling out of my stuff?" Don't worry if some of your brainstormed ideas seem silly—sometimes the best ideas come from off-the-wall ideas.

For example, a class held a brainstorming session on how to move a very heavy table. One of the students suggested tying balloons to it and floating it above the ground. This idea sounded silly at first, but it gave the class an idea that worked. They used air pressure and a hovercraft to move the table.

The first step in effective brainstorming starts out with one person recording everyone's ideas a quickly as possible—without judging the ideas. The second step involves looking at the brainstormed list for potential solutions and narrowing the list down to three favorites. The third step of brainstorming is to analyze those three solutions and decide which one to create. This process should include sketching and researching each one to learn what materials and supplies you might need, as well as figuring out how hard each might be to build. By the end of step three, you should have decided on a solution to move forward with.

Brainstorming works best when you come up with lots of ideas and record all of them, even the silly ones!

Try This

- Share your notes from Chapter 3 with a friend, parent, teacher, librarian, or someone from the makerspace. Discuss your ideas and goals, and then ask them to brainstorm solutions to this problem with you.
- Write a list of all the solutions during the brainstorming session.
- Use a phone or tablet to record your brainstorming session and then take notes from the video.
- Decide which solution you're going to act on.

CHAPTER FIVE

Prototype

Now it's time to take the idea you decided on in your brainstorming session and test it out. **Prototypes** are meant to be early models of a design and should be taken apart and reworked multiple times. Your prototype will likely go through many **iterations** before becoming the final plan. Depending on your ideas, you may want to look at your alarm prototype as two projects:

1. The electronic components making up the circuit and switch
2. The non-electronic part, such as a box with a hinge, a container with a secret compartment, a pretend diary, a clothespin switch, or some unique invention nobody has thought of before

For your electronic components, use what's available to you from your home, library, classroom, or makerspace. This might include an electronics starter kit like littleBits, Snap Circuits, Squishy Circuits, or, if you're advanced, a microcontroller such as an Arduino. For the non-electronic part of your prototype, you can use cardboard, popsicle sticks, tape, and hot glue—or you could use another building kit you already have. Don't spend money on making and remaking a prototype. Cheap and fast materials work best!

You might want to use the LEGOs you already have to make your prototype.

Try This

- Experiment with your electronics kit. Build a few sample projects following the directions in the kit before you start your prototype. Once you're comfortable with the kit and the components, then you can build your first prototype circuit.
- An option here is to decide if you want to build any non-electronic parts of your project separately and then combine the two parts together. For example, you might make part of your prototype out of LEGO pieces and part out of pieces from a littleBits kit, and then combine them.
- Take your time. Even though this is a prototype, it shouldn't be overly messy. Too much mess will make it hard for people to see what your invention is designed to do.

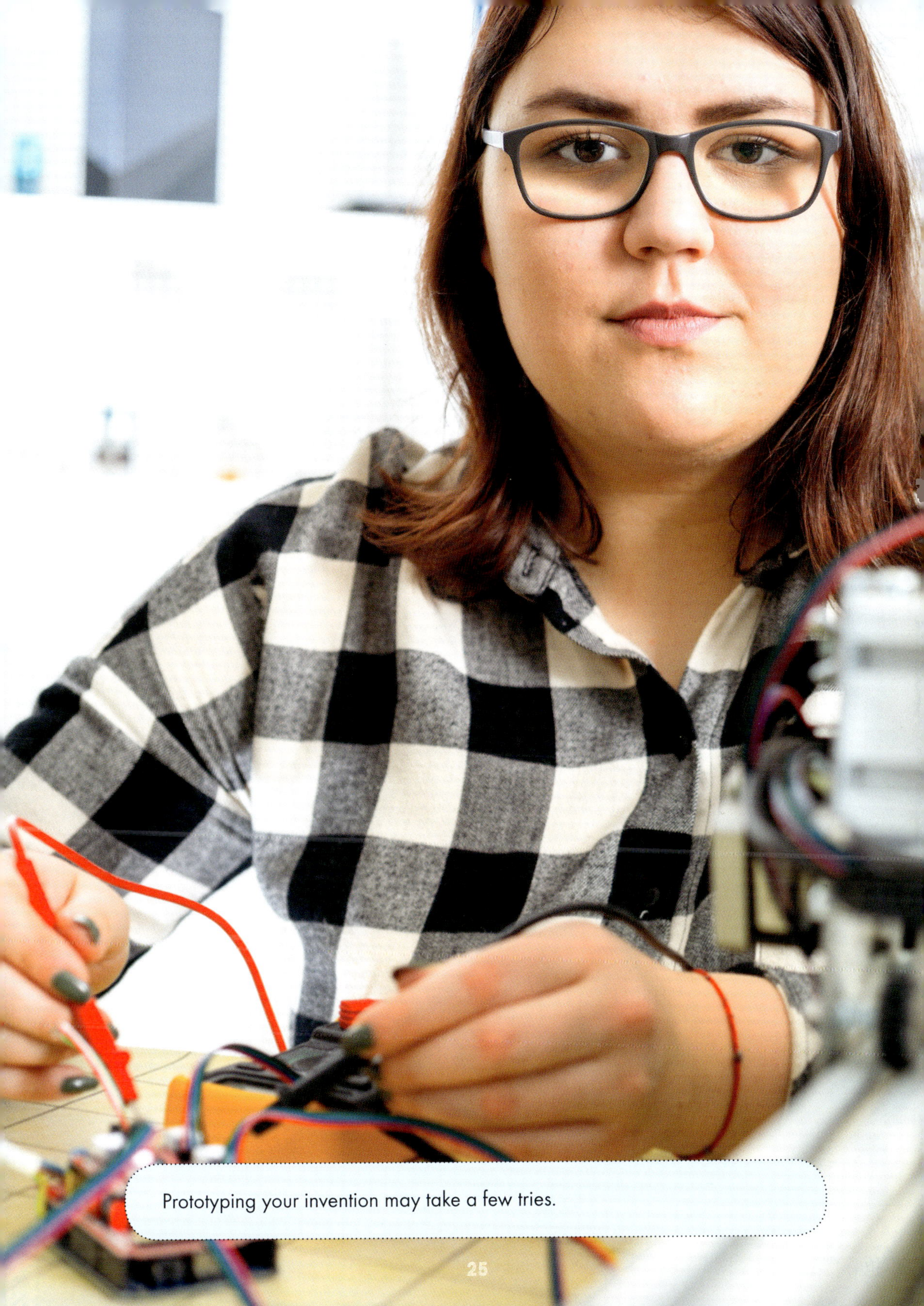

Prototyping your invention may take a few tries.

CHAPTER SIX

Test, Adjust, Test Again

Test your prototype and see if it works. It is normal if your first attempt doesn't work—that's why we used inexpensive materials and things that can easily be reworked. Professional engineers make multiple prototypes, and you should too. It's all part of the design process!

Each time you build and test your prototype, take notes and photos of things that worked and things that didn't work. Engineers often learn the most while fixing projects that don't work or have broken. When something breaks, go back to the setup that worked last and see if you can figure out what went wrong. Don't forget to observe your photos along the way—they may give you a hint about what went wrong. Add all of this new information to your designer's notebook. It should reflect your thinking at every stage of the project.

Try This

- Build and modify your prototype until you are happy with it.
- Take your working prototype to people you interviewed during the research phase of your project and have them test it out. The people who test your design and give you **feedback** are called **beta** testers.
- Make notes about how your beta testers interact with your project and what difficulties they have along the way.
- Ask your beta testers for feedback about your project. Remember to take constructive criticism well. It can be difficult to have someone tell you how your invention could be better. So before you ask for feedback, you may want to say, "I worked hard on this project, so please keep your feedback constructive but kind." Some questions you may want to ask your beta testers are:
    - Does my prototype work the way you expected it to?
    - Was my prototype difficult to use? If so, how?
    - If you could change something to make it work better, what would it be and why?
- Take your notes and feedback, and rework your prototype. Repeat this process until you feel your project works the way you want it to.

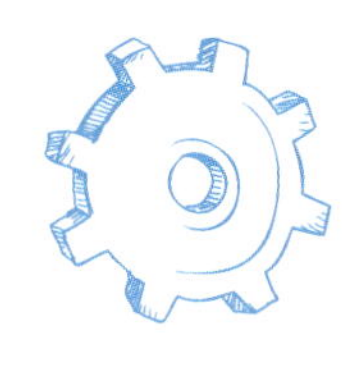

CHAPTER SEVEN

Implement!

Congratulations! You are now at the final stage of your project's development. It is time to build your final product, using everything you've gathered in your designer's notebook and what you envisioned during the design process. You may want to seek help from a parent, the librarian, or someone at the makerspace. The first time you use new materials to build this final version, you may discover some small design problems. This is okay. You have the experience you need to tweak your project and get it to work correctly. After all, at this point you are an expert!

Try This

- Set up your final project, take a few pictures, and include them in your designer's notebook. Add any relevant notes about your photos in the notebook.
- Take your final project and your designer's notebook to everyone who helped you. Show them the process you went through and your resulting invention.

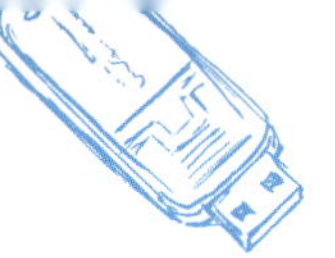

Learn More

Books

Cook, Eric. *Prototyping*. Ann Arbor, MI: Cherry Lake Publishing, 2015.

Lovett, Amber. *LittleBits*. Ann Arbor, MI: Cherry Lake Publishing, 2016.

Websites

DK Find Out!
https://www.dkfindout.com/us/search/electricity
Find out more about many topics related to electricity.

Squishy Circuits
https://squishycircuits.com
Learn about how play dough is used to teach the basics of electrical circuits.

YouTube—How to Make a Simple Door Alarm
https://www.youtube.com/watch?v=_KcsJ-fojJM
Watch a video about making a door alarm with a simple circuit.

Glossary

beta (BAY-tuh) an early version of a product, such as software

brainstorming (BRAYN-storm-ing) thinking of as many ideas as possible

design problem (dih-ZINE PRAH-bluhm) something that doesn't work well that you think you can make better

design thinking (dih-ZINE THINGK-ing) a process for studying, testing, and solving problems

designers (dih-ZYE-nurz) people who organize ideas and images into useful and attractive things or sequences

designer's notebook (dih-ZYE-nurz NOTE-buk) a small book of paper in which inventors and designers keep notes, sketches, inspirations, and photos of their design process

electrical engineering (ih-LEK-trik-uhl en-juh-NEER-ing) a field in which people solve problems using electricity and electrical components

electricity (ih-lek-TRIS-ih-tee) the free flow of electrons; when electricity is used in a circuit, it is the controlled flow of electrons

feedback (FEED-bak) the information you get back after doing or saying something

focus (FOH-kuhs) to narrow down to one idea or really concentrate on one thing

input (IN-put) what goes into a system

iterations (ih-tuh-RAY-shuhnz) versions or refinements of a prototype that get you closer to a final design

makers (MAY-kurz) people who design and build or craft things for enjoyment or to solve problems

makerspace (MAY-kur-spays) a space with tools, materials, and people with expertise who collaborate and help others build and make things

microcontrollers (mye-kroh-kuhn-TROHL-urz) programmable circuit boards used in advanced electrical design

output (OUT-put) what comes out of a system

patterns (PAT-urnz) when the same thing or similar thing shows up more than once

prototypes (PROH-tuh-tipes) "first drafts" of inventions

schematic (skeh-MAT-ik) a graphic sketch or outline

synthesize (SIN-thuh-size) to look at a lot of ideas and figure out what the big picture is or what the patterns are

Index

Peter Pasque is an advocate for creativity in the classroom. He believes that learning should be a by-product of discovery and innovation. Peter has conducted workshops across Michigan and presented at numerous state and international educational technology conferences. He has worked to organize numerous Mini Maker Faires. Peter is a lecturer at the University of Michigan School of Education.